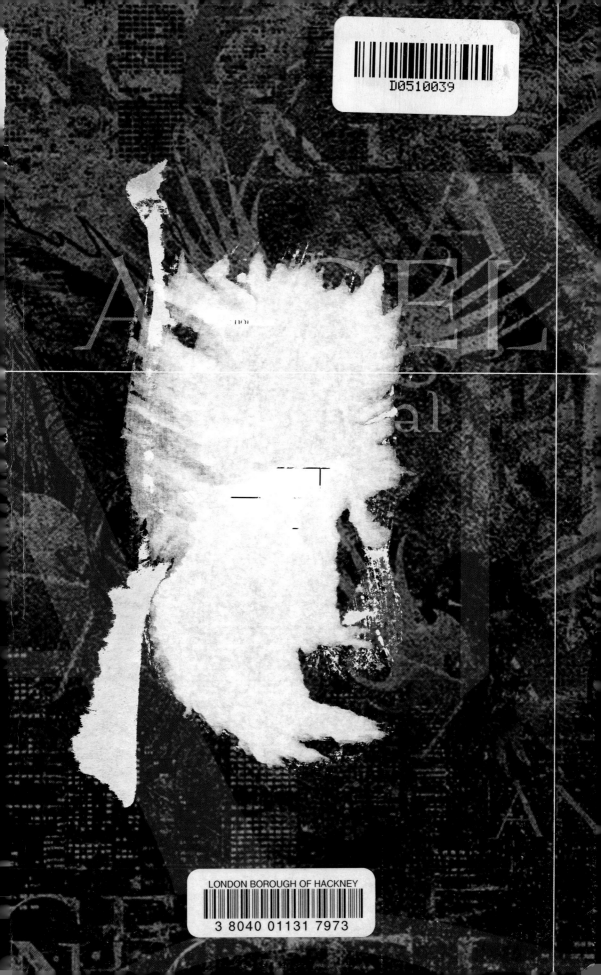

D0510039

ANGEL™

Autumnal

based on the television series
created by
JOSS WHEDON and DAVID GREENWALT

by
CHRISTOPHER GOLDEN, TOM SNIEGOSKI,
CHRISTIAN ZANIER, and ERIC POWELL

with
MARVIN MARIANO, ANDREW PEPOY,
MARK HEIKE, CLAYTON BROWN,
CHRIS IVY, DEREK FRIDOLFS,
JASON MOORE, LEE LOUGHRIDGE,
CLEM ROBINS, and PAT BROSSEAU

Titan Books

publisher
MIKE RICHARDSON

editor
SCOTT ALLIE
with ADAM GALLARDO and MIKE CARRIGLITTO

collection designers
KEITH WOOD and DARCY HOCKETT

art director
MARK COX

Special thanks to
DEBBIE OLSHAN at Fox Licensing,
CAROLINE KALLAS and GEORGE SNYDER at
Buffy the Vampire Slayer.

Published by
Titan Books
144 Southwark Street
London SE1 OUP

First edition: December 2001
ISBN: 1-84023-396-6

1 3 5 7 9 10 8 6 4 2

Printed in Italy
These stories take place during **Angel's** first season.

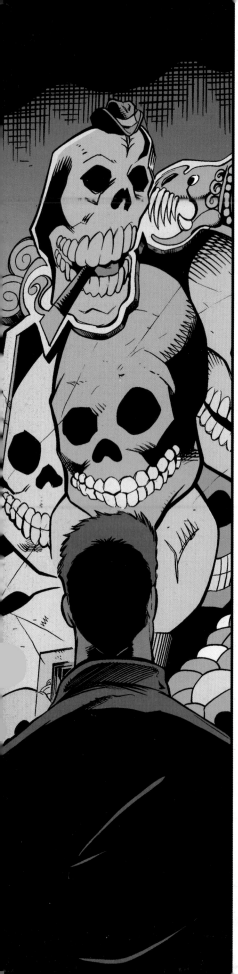

SKREEEEK
SKREEEE

...PLEASE... SOMEBODY HELP ME...

WASSA- MADDUH LITTLE GIRL? WHY YA CRYIN'?

THE END

ALIENS

LABYRINTH
Woodring • Plunkett
136-page color paperback
ISBN: 1-85286-844-9

NIGHTMARE ASYLUM
(formerly Aliens: Book Two)
Verheiden • Beauvais
112-page color paperback
ISBN: 1-85286-765-5

OUTBREAK
(formerly Aliens: Book One)
Verheiden • Nelson
168-page color paperback
ISBN: 1-85286-756-6

ALIENS VS PREDATOR

ALIENS VS PREDATOR
Stradley • Norwood • Warner
176-page color paperback
ISBN: 1-85286-413-3

**THE DEADLIEST
OF THE SPECIES**
Claremont • Guice • Barreto
320-page color paperback
ISBN: 1-85286-953-4

WAR
Various
200-page color paperback
ISBN: 1-85286-703-5

ETERNAL
Edginton • Maleev
88-page color paperback
ISBN: 1-84023-111-4

**ALIENS VS. PREDATOR
VS. TERMINTAOR**
Schultz • Ruby • Ivy
96-page color paperback
ISBN: 1-84023-313-3

ANGEL

THE HOLLOWER
Golden • Gomez • Florea
88-page color paperback
ISBN: 1-84023-163-7

SURROGATES
Golden •Zanier •
Owens • Gomez
80-page color paperback
ISBN: 1-84023-234-X

BUFFY THE VAMPIRE SLAYER

THE DUST WALTZ
Brereton • Gomez
80-page color paperback
ISBN: 1-84023-057-6

THE REMAINING SUNLIGHT
Watson • Van Meter •
Bennett • Ross
88-page color paperback
ISBN: 1-84023-078-9

THE ORIGIN
Golden • Brereton •
Bennett • Ketcham
80-page color paperback
ISBN: 1-84023-105-X

RING OF FIRE
Petrie • Sook
80-page color paperback
ISBN: 1-84023-200-5

UNINVITED GUESTS
Watson • Brereton •
Gomez • Florea
96-page color paperback
ISBN: 1-84023-140-8

BAD BLOOD
Watson • Bennett • Ketcham
88-page color paperback
ISBN: 1-84023-179-3

CRASH TEST DEMONS
Watson • Richards • Pimentel
88-page color paperback
ISBN: 1-84023-199-8

PALE REFLECTIONS
Watson • Richards • Pimentel
96-page color paperback
ISBN: 1-84023-236-6

THE BLOOD OF CARTHAGE
Golden • Richards • Pimentel
128-page color paperback
ISBN: 1-84023-281-1

STAR WARS

**BOBA FETT: ENEMY OF
THE EMPIRE**
Wagner • Gibson • Nadeau
112-page color paperback
ISBN: 1-84023-125-4

BOUNTY HUNTERS
Stradley • Truman • Schultz •
Mangels •Nadeau • Rubi • Saltares
112-page color paperback
ISBN: 1-84023-238-2

CHEWBACCA
Macan • Various
96-page color paperback
ISBN: 1-84023-274-9

CRIMSON EMPIRE
Richardson • Stradley •
Gulacy • Russell
160-page color paperback
ISBN: 1-84023-006-1

CRIMSON EMPIRE II
Richardson • Stradley •
Gulacy • Emberlin
160-page color paperback
ISBN: 1-84023-126-2

DARK EMPIRE
Veitch • Kennedy
184-page color paperback
ISBN: 1-84023-098-3

DARK EMPIRE II
Veitch • Kennedy
168-page color paperback
ISBN: 1-84023-099-1

**EPISODE I
THE PHANTOM MENACE**
Gilroy • Damaggio • Williamson
112-page color paperback
ISBN: 1-84023-025-8

EPISODE I ADVENTURES
152-page color paperback
ISBN: 1-84023-177-7

JEDI ACADEMY – LEVIATHAN
Anderson • Carrasco • Heike
96-page color paperback
ISBN: 1-84023-138-6

THE LAST COMMAND
Baron • Biukovic • Shanower
144-page color paperback
ISBN: 1-84023-007-X

**MARA JADE:
BY THE EMPEROR'S HAND**
Zahn • Stackpole • Ezquerra
144-page color paperback
ISBN: 1-84023-011-8

PRELUDE TO REBELLION
Strnad • Winn • Jones
144-page color paperback
ISBN: 1-84023-139-4

SHADOWS OF THE EMPIRE
Wagner • Plunkett • Russell
160-page color paperback
ISBN: 1-84023-009-6

**SHADOWS OF THE EMPIRE:
EVOLUTION**
Perry • Randall • Simmons
120-page color paperback
ISBN: 1-84023-135-1

**TALES OF THE JEDI:
DARK LORDS OF THE SITH**
Veitch • Anderson • Gossett
160-page color paperback
ISBN: 1-84023-129-7

**TALES OF THE JEDI:
FALL OF THE SITH**
Anderson • Heike • Carrasco, Jr.
136-page color paperback
ISBN: 1-84023-012-6

**TALES OF THE JEDI: THE
GOLDEN AGE OF THE SITH**
Anderson • Gossett •
Carrasco • Heike
144-page color paperback
ISBN: 1-84023-000-2

**TALES OF THE JEDI:
THE SITH WAR**
152-page color paperback
ISBN: 1-84023-130-0

UNION
Stackpole • Teranishi • Chuckry
96-page color paperback
ISBN: 1-84023-233-1

VADER'S QUEST
Macan • Gibbons • McKie
96-page color paperback
ISBN: 1-84023-149-1

**X-WING ROGUE SQUADRON:
THE WARRIOR PRINCESS**
Stackpole • Tolson •
Nadeau • Ensign
96-page color paperback
ISBN: 1-85286-997-6

**X-WING ROGUE SQUADRON:
REQUIEM FOR A ROGUE**
Stackpole • Strnad • Erskine
112-page color paperback
ISBN: 1-84023-026-6

**X-WING ROGUE SQUADRON:
IN THE EMPIRE'S SERVICE**
Stackpole • Nadeau • Ensign
96-page color paperback
ISBN: 1-84023-008-8

**X-WING ROGUE SQUADRON:
BLOOD AND HONOR**
Stackpole • Crespo •
Hall • Johnson
96-page color paperback
ISBN: 1-84023-010-X

**X-WING ROGUE SQUADRON:
MASQUERADE**
Stackpole •Johnson • Martin
96-page color paperback
ISBN: 1-84023-201-3

**X-WING ROGUE SQUADRON:
MANDATORY RETIREMENT**
Stackpole • Crespo • Nadeau
96-page color paperback
ISBN: 1-84023-239-0

**All publications are available through most good bookshops or
direct from our mail-order service at Titan Books. For a free
graphic-novels catalogue or to order, telephone 01536 764 646
with your credit-card details or contact Titan Books Mail Order,
Unit 6 Pipewell Industrial Estate, Desborough, Kettering,Northants,
NN14 2SW, quoting reference AAUT/GN.**